# FRED BEAR and FRIENDS

First published in Great Britain in 2007 by ticktock Media Ltd.,
Unit 2, Orchard Business Centre, North Farm Road,
Tunbridge Wells, Kent, TN2 3XF

*author: Melanie Joyce*
*ticktock project editor: Julia Adams*
*ticktock project designer: Emma Randall*
*ticktock image co-ordinator: Lizzie Knowles*

We would like to thank: Colin Beer, Tim Bones, Rebecca Clunes, James Powell, Dr. Naima Browne,
Ann Radford and all the staff and pupils at Buxted C of E Primary School, and St Luke's Infant School, Tunbridge Wells

ISBN 978 1 84696 506 7 pbk

Printed in China

A CIP catalogue record for this book is available from the British Library. 

Picture credits
t=top, b=bottom, c=centre, l=left, r=right, bg=background
All photography by Colin Beer of JL Allwork Photography except for the following: Shutterstock: 23tl

Every effort has been made to trace the copyright holders, and we apologise in advance for any unintentional omissions.
We would be pleased to insert the appropriate acknowledgements in any subsequent edition of this publication.

# Meet Fred Bear and Friends

Fred

Arthur

Betty

# Also starring...

Today is Betty's first day at school. She is very excited.

"I'm sure you will love school," says Fred.

Fred, Arthur, Jess and Betty all leave their house to walk to school together.

When the bears arrive at school, Betty sees her friend Dolly.

Dolly is starting school today, too. Dolly and Betty meet their new teacher, Miss Jones.

Betty hears a bell:

**'Drrrring!'**

The bell is a sign that a lesson is about to start.

Betty follows Miss Jones inside the school.

Miss Jones asks everyone to hang up their coats in the cloakroom.

Then they all go to the classroom and sit down.

First, Miss Jones calls all the pupils' names so she knows who is there. "Betty...?" "Yes, Miss Jones," says Betty.

In the first lesson, they find out about shapes. Betty and Dolly really like this lesson.

In the second lesson, Betty and Dolly practise counting. Betty counts the blue shapes on the board: "One, two, three, four," she says.

The bell rings again:

**'Drrring!'**

It is break time. Everyone goes to play outside.

Betty and Dolly make new friends.

"Hello, I am Max."

"Hello, I am Alice. Would you like to play a game?"

Betty, Dolly, Max and Alice play lots of games at break time. Dolly loves playing hopscotch.

**Fred Bear says...**

Break time is a great time to make new friends. Then you can play your favourite games with your new friends!

After the break, Miss Jones takes the class to the sports hall.

The class play a ball game. Betty is good at catching. It is her favourite game.

After the sports lesson, Betty is feeling hungry. Now it is lunchtime.

Alice, Dolly and Betty sit together to have their lunch in the canteen.

In the afternoon, the class do lots of different things. Betty and Dolly draw pictures and then they do some puzzles in a book.

Later, Miss Jones reads the class a story. This is really good fun, because Miss Jones does all the different voices.

The bell rings.

**'Drrring!'**

It's time to go home.

Fred, Jess and Arthur are waiting for Betty at the school gate.

They all go home together.

At home Betty plays schools with Fred, Jess and Arthur. Betty is the teacher.

"I made lots of new friends at school." says Betty.

Betty cannot wait to go back to school again tomorrow.

"I love my new school!" says Betty.

# Match the shapes!

Betty loved finding out about different shapes. These are the shapes she learned.

square

rectangle

triangle

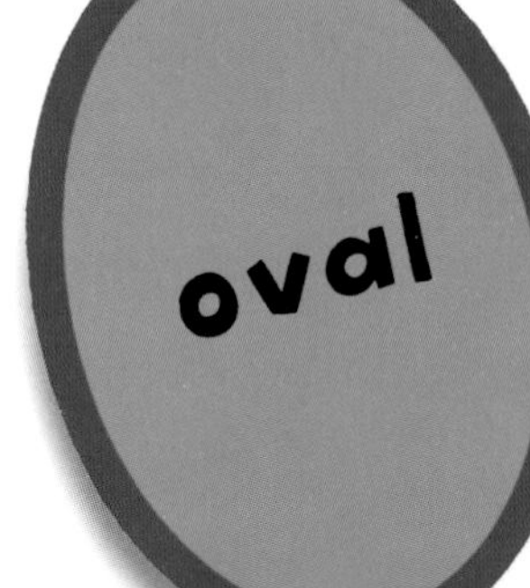


diamond

Here are some of the things Betty saw at school.

Can you say what shapes they are?

# Fun with numbers!

Dolly loves playing hopscotch at break time. Can you match the white numbers to those on the hopscotch grid?

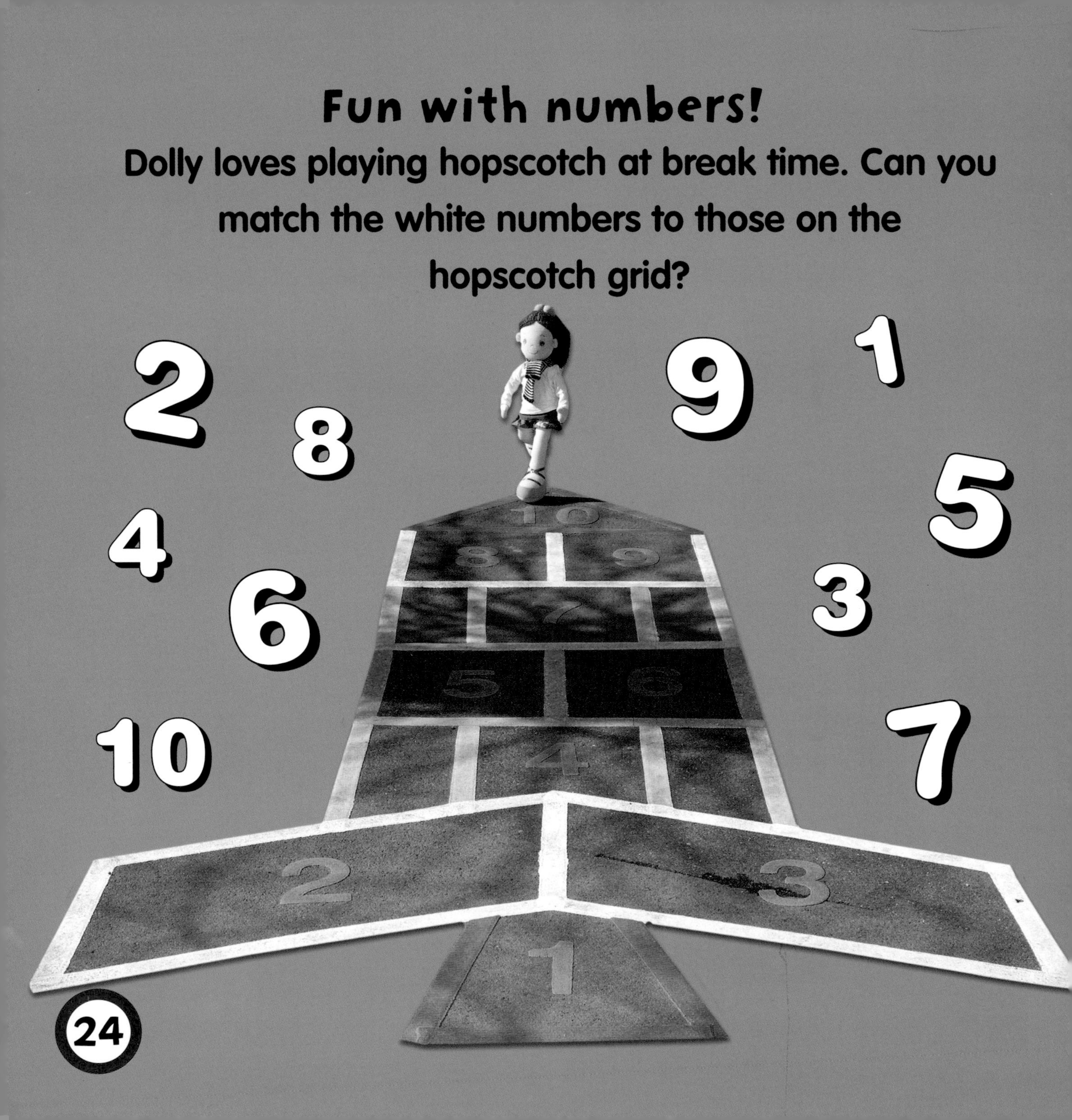